SHORE LOVE

and that cut, Cat

MATT TALLBOY

**Shore Love
and that cut, Cat**

First published in Australia by Matt Tallboy 2025
tallboybooks@gmail.com

A catalogue record for this
book is available from the
National Library of Australia

ISBN: 978-1-7635192-2-0 (pbk)
ISBN: 978-1-7635192-3-7 (ebk)

Typesetting and design by Publicious Book Publishing
Published with the assistance of Publicious Book Publishing
www.publicious.com.au

Cover photography by Aleksandr Ozerov (shutterstock) © 2025
Internal images by Copilot © 2025

Let's have a better world.

Contents

Shore Love
A Lesson in Communication

I ONCE WENT COURTING, by the sea.

"Is this shore love?" she asked of me.

I said yes.

Upon which … verily, she gave of herself to me quite willingly and freely, on the dune.

And there we lay on the sandhill, under a lover's full moon.

On my own performance: I thought quite sound.

That which moved beneath her, was *not* the ground, … and

Naturally, she was breathless … delighted.

She said her bosom was heaving, over-excited.

Amongst her many mumblings, I heard 'bosoms,' so …
to her breasts, I spoke aloud my thought, "I love you two,"

… which had her jump like a kangaroo!

BUT, MY BRAIN WAVES evolving as they ought,

burgeoning from a tiny *seed* to a wriggling *embryo* of thought,

and finally, a pulsing, blue-ish-pinking,

living *foetus* of deep, considered thinking.

Void of doubt and all confusion.

Next, I'm *in labour*, rejoicing in the *deliverance* of one,
and only one conclusion:

Namely: *Our shore love was not even on the beach!*

Ergo, how can it be *shore*? The water line was far beyond a sprinter's reach,

and we were way, way, way up in the dune.

Now not spurred on by any want for needless hurting, I birthed my brain-bubble baby boy, by boldly blurting, "I spoke too soon,

I've thought quite hard on that … shore line,

… I was far from shore in my own mind!

And so … without wanting a huge 'to-do',

I must say now, my love to you,

while … *close* to shore, was *not* … sincerely … completely … shorely,"

… after which she cried and acted poorly.

Any willpower she had for keeping tact near shore was plainly lacking, …

And with one single, *almighty smite* … connecting with profound impact, my eye was hurt and quickly blacking.

My conscious state best described as semi,

And thinking… my *birth* of thought, while close to shore, may have been a wee bit *premie*.

WHO WILL SOLVE the mystery of women?!?!?

I've had one good lesson, surely given.

Delivered by a girlie fist! Hardened … Nay! *Tempered*, by the uncorked fury previously bottled up tight, embedded deep within a woman's … scorn,

Converting her to an Amazon Samson! (… except not so tall & also not the hairy Samson, the one that's freshly shorn.)

Even now, years later, I can still but wonder in depth what-for and why, as I still (as yet fruitless) try,

To see the world … from the woman's point of view, albeit looking through … my *one* remaining eye.

YES … IT IS BY *woman* I have been well taught,

from conception right through to the very birth of thought,

To ponder on the thought *abortion*,

Or risk giving *birth* to thought without due caution.

For I am man … the *father* of that foolish spoken thought, airborne.

From within my quick mind, (which is really an empty, barren box, … *masquerading* to me as a fertile *womb* for productive thought, well … from *this* two-faced place) my baby thought has been wrenched … and torn.

Spoken words! Born …

Words, which … hang in the air like the maiden flight of a downy bird,

Only to spiral down to the ground,

When the faintest uttered, *whispered* sound,

I make, may be drawn out, gutted, twisted around,

into what … she heard.

IT IS JUST SO, I have learned, that when walking hand-in-hand,

With view to spoon or woo, until the sweet surrender, so tender on … that *rasping* sand …

To avoid mixed up feelings, make any amorous dealings … clearly … written …

or learn to love the hurt you gain, *embrace* your new best friend, Mister Endless-Pain, who seems to come … with being … *smitten.*

And don't stamp me with unfair, misanthropic brandings,

Near sure, 'tis a far, far better world, a world with no misunderstandings,

… about tangled, knees-and-elbows, love.

That thought which sparks in disparate minds,

Fuels different fires of desperate kinds …

of confusing, controlling, contractual, consensual,

Always consensual … ways of making love.

Always consensual … ways of making love.

YOU MAY WELL ASK, would I chance my hand …
to find the love I need, near shore again?

But if you had seen, what I've seen, with my very *own eye*,

or stepped a mile in my shoes, … in my dim world …
of *peripheral blindness* and *optical pain* …

Then you would easily, plainly and clearly see!

… (in ironic, stark contrast to foreshore-loveless me.)

And hitherto, even you, would give joyous *birth* to the postulate, that so close to shore,

I can love no more!

FOR I HAVE BEEN cut by the claw … of the lioness,

(With regrets, if only I had cared less for I and more for eyeless, I guess.)

And from a cat*, 'the first cut is the deepest,' and sharper than the serpent's tooth,

with shore-close proximity any cut delivered with venom is salt in my wound, without any ruth.

… (ruthless) …

BUT I SEEK NOT your pity, before you I stand,

A simple and proud, some say aloof, monocular man,

In possession of a one-track mind without change. Foolish romantics have tried,

Believe me … I would surrender my Cartier monocle not to be so one-eyed.

But of this I am certain, I have unwithering resolve, I am definite.

With extreme governance, there is no more! Cock-on sure!

There is no love for me … by the sea,

… by the sea.

"All that's not read … *can* signal green,

But when we average what's said, it should be what we mean."

*APPENDIX TO SHORE LOVE
ON THAT CUT, CAT

NOW CAT, on the deepest first cut.

I do say tut-tut.

Because you say *"the deepest"*, which is *comparative*, so,

Cat, you leave me … many logical ways I could go,

Now do pay attention, and Cat, don't leave your mind shut.

Assuming I've had my tragic first cut;

… if say, another (with a blade) took to me as an axe takes to wood,

I should just lie back there, and relax there, I should?

OR … A SURGEON is about to have a real, good go at my heart.

I say "doctor … mister … mate!

Wait!

Before you scrub, gown up and start,

Cat says, *the first cut is deepest,* and … I've already had one of those,

(I had a skin cancer cut from my nose.)

So this time, go in,

No deeper than skin,

to clear all of that,

life-threatening fat, which is blocking my hose."

FOR CAT, NO OTHER CUT is ever so deep.

(By your words, the mantra to keep.)

But it's too easy Cat,

to mount a more *formal* case to counter with that.

And I do note here the specific type of cut (conveniently) *not* mentioned by you.

I guess, so easy to *not* write that Cat, … from your ivory temple, up there, in Katmandu.

But we're all here in the … *real world*, Cat.

And now I'm at the (metaphorical) crease, and it's my turn to bat.

THE CUTTER JOHN-B

THE BLACKSMITHS OF CHILE pulled out all the stops,

To get bright colours into their drab shops.

Now, in Chile the blacksmiths … love their ballet,

they'd squeal with delight for an Oscar Wilde play,

Wear pink overalls,

Enough to cover their smalls,

they party at night, work their forge in the day.

They live their lives proud, unashamed.

They find respect for all people and hold on to the dream that we *all* … do the same.

T'WAS A LOVE OF SHOPPING took our smithies to vibrant Brazil.

It was there, that they found … *the great rainbow anvil.*

An eye-catching *anvil*, a Roy G Biv design,

With all rainbow colours, and a side-mounted holder, for a bottle of wine.

Feeling a bit naughty, they ordered forty, to ship home by boat 'round fearsome Cape Horn.

And dockside, a rainbow cutter, ready to sail, so scrumptiously perfect, all planets aligned, it's "cast-off" at dawn!

At the helm, Captain Morse. Scrubbing decks fore-and-aft, were his brave, busy crew.

All, identifying as men, would get those *rainbow anvils*, back round the Horn, next morn, t'would be easy to do.

So at sun-up, with Morse in command of the cutter, John-B,

And with cargo hold *full* of the rainbow Roy-G's,

and two sheets on the mizzen, they set off to sea.

OUT OF RIO, and south down the coast.

A light zephyr puffing the sails, calm conditions to boast.

Morse too, had unjangled nerve right through, to match the sailing conditions.

Determined to see this cargo safely off, to blacksmithing fruition.

So, with one huge swig of rum from his salty hip-flask,

He pondered the *vital importance* of his one, simple task.

For in Chile, gay rights had been lost and were drifting.

He knew full well, these *anvils* for gay smiths were symbolic, uplifting.

Get them safe round the Horn,

And revolution is born!

Maybe what's needed to start attitudes shifting.

NOW WHEN MORSE left Rio, he never ever thought he would have to be brave.

A fair-weather sailor, he never ever … had to *cut* … through a wave.

But down round the Horn,

is where *real* sailors are born …

So, for the first wave, for that virgin cutter to cut,

John-B was prepped, bilge-pumps checked, passageways shut.

Morse gave that crew, a good talking to;

"Men! Men! Identifying as Men! Time and again,

we've heard,

the promise … the word, that

The first cut is the deepest, so shimmy up that mast, faint heart be saved!

One gold doubloon! To the man in the 'nest' who points me that wave,

Which towers out of the sea, to test the cutter John-B.

Stake your claim to your gold, by shouting *'thar she blows!'*

Because from rudder to figurehead, everyone knows,

when we cut that *deepest* of waves, bearing sou-west,

You'll have earned that anchor, inked … on your … beautiful breast."

THEN MORSE SET a course to the wildest of squalls,

Found that ... *deepest* of waves with the highest of walls.

And through it, he cut.

A good theory, but ...

halfway through, the cutter just stalls! ... ...

Morse and his crew … … *had more life to sail through.*

Crew, cargo, cutter John-B,

And one gold doubloon, *all* lost at sea.

But what's really gold is the irony … in iron. If they only knew …

uplifting anvils … would sink like … they do.

Men of the John B Crew

Jed

Hugo

Brian

Matthew

EACH YEAR on the anniversary of the John-B sinking,

Blacksmiths hold hands, take time off their tinking,

To mourn the loss of those anvils, numbering two score.

[And also, some flamingo sledgehammer handles, a bargain on sale] *now* at Davy Jones' locker, on the sea floor.

They bow heads and chant a Chilean, gay,

blacksmithing verse, always recited … *united* that day:

"WE, WHO MEND WAGONS, bang hammers,

We're typecast on screen as big, simple *hombres*, with impeccable manners.

Senoritas, senors! Our singleted, broad shoulders are yours,

To forge you a plough or temper your rail.

Coke-up the furnace right now, for a *party of flame* to the nail.

To the beat of Motown, our forceps cool down.

You'll hear Y-M-C-A … in our fab, little workshop all day.

We were born full of love and perfectly gay.

With horseshoes turned up, lucky and proud, enabled and needing, to shout out aloud: We were all … *born this way!*

Unafraid and awake, still unconverted to straight, by swinging a hammer.

So stand with us now, under our pink highly held, black-smithery banner.

Give us the nod,

We'll get *tus caballos* all shod,

be they stallion or filly or … choose not to say.

We're up from the Horn, and through us is born, the spirit of Chile.

Strong, blacksmithing, and proud to be gay."

CUT VERSUS CAT

CAT, WHAT MORE can I say?

Except …

Cunard Line, want back their vessel!

Which went 'water-ship down' like a rabbit, attempting the backstroke, having just swallowed a mortar and pestle.

It's quite a to-do.

They've set free their slobbering lawyers … they're coming for you.

AND IT SEEMS to me Cat, like the whole *industry of cuts* could now file, for libel,

So Cat, you can stay on your prayer-mat, clutching your bible,

But expect letters which threaten to see you in court.

With one word "deepest" … the problems you've brought!

FROM PEOPLE as varied as; road cutting workers,

Kitchenhands, paid pittance to cut the frankfurters,

Chefs, surgeons, lumberjacks, editors,

Those rich, cut-shouting movie-directors.

Greenkeepers carefully keeping a green.

Sweat-shop workers, trapped by poor wages, scissoring cloth near a sewing machine.

Burley sheep shearers sharpening shears,

And barbers who snip and clip the hairs in your ears.

Kids who cut school or just cut and run.

Those who cut corners to get the job done.

Bank-robbers taking their cut of the loot,

And owls, nothing about cutting but they should be included, they do give a hoot.

Speakers, who shorten their talks to cut to the chase.

And florists, snipping their stalks for an American vase.

Phone operators, who cut off your calls,

And bull castrators … who … wear overalls.

Bosses, saving on wages by cutting their staff.

Magicians, who saw pretty ladies in half.

The (estates of the) crew of the cutter, John-B!

Who knew what to do but were all lost at sea!

And … those in overalls, all pink and frilly!

The sweet ever-lovin' gay blacksmiths of Chile!

COUPLES IN LOVE, this day newly wed,

Busting and eager for that lusting in bed,

Now strutting for cameras and cutting their cakes,

But would stop all their slicing, through icing and put on the brakes, …

To join all these people singing, as one, *well-worded* songs.

Music, Cat, aimed back, at poor pitiful you, its a public review, righting the wrongs.

Together united, ready, and angry, *determined* to fight it,

in a drawn out, exhaustive, class-action suit.

All of them wanting a song of retraction, to boot!

Cat, your beautiful, musical life would quickly unravel,

with the wood-on-wood sound, of the pound … … of the gavel.

AND NOW HEAR ME Cat, in full simulated,

barrister-babble, always much-hated.

(To be read with added pompous, arrogant tone)

And picture yourself, Cat, cuffed in a dock, sitting, all on your own.

(But not by yourself, the bailiff is there), you're sobbing, and hearing;

"If it pleases the court, my case (in Cut versus Cat) is nearing,

Climax, as it hinges and tracks, to critical point two:

[Point one had been done, was cutter John-B, all hands lost at sea,

Now, another point to get through, critical point two]

Your Honour, imagine, slicing one's food, and take good time to rue,

That one can only use cuts becoming progressively more *shallow*.

The result? Any food on one's plate, lies there, all … fallow.

On this, I'm utterly un-clued.

How sir, to cut completely right through, one's *meant-to-be* edible food?

So little to eat! *Except* what's eaten *post* …

first cut and *pre*-cut number two, leaving *most* …

Meal on the plate. So to eat,

Your veggies *or* meat,

yes Cat, for the pure, clean vegetarian,

or like me the common carnivorous contrarian …"

[CAT, PICTURE NOW THIS, upper-class titters reverb 'round the court, even the beak,

himself not so slender, and a keen lover of tender, medium-rare meat.

Cat you could 'I object', but to what … dry, legal humour?

Maybe if you laughed just a little bit yourself … but your happy life Cat, is now, barely a rumour,

and now *comparatively* worse than the one you had tunefully planned,

For, as a jocular wig, I would now have that court eating cake, from the palm of my hand.

… and through all the laughter (aimed squarely at you),

An eager QC could twist the knife further, with yet more to do …]

"IT FOLLOWS, MILORD, that the second cut, and third, and so on, and so on,

Should be *equally* deep, which makes that one, word written, by the defendant … just wrong.

So at behest of my ravaged clients, the whole cutting crew,

There is but one more request of defiance, the *comparative* best I can do.

I'm filing, Milord, for top compensation. *E pluribus unum maximus!*

Let's get my clients home in a limo Milord … *not* on the bus.

And Milord, we are … seeking costs. You do have the power,

To grant my clients, who are suffering at best, that simple request, my face-to-face comes at a million an hour.

... plus photocopying, the Chambers charge that without fail,

and *sundries*, of course, like each *second* my clients pay rent ... for those hours I've spent, on the ... e-mail.

And ... there are 'expenses', Milord, like lunch,

at the club with my shrewd legal team,

Essential to brief my chambers bunch,

and digest that brief *rightly* with brain food like peaches ... and cream.

YOUR HONOUR! OUR LADY *Justitia* weighs the evidence and holds up those scales,

To remind us, we do the same. We don't just tap our feet, to the beat, of fanciful, *comparative* tales.

And the law does give every dog, truly, his day,

But artistic crime *from a cat*, deserves creative time, and should not and will not, be paid.

And to the defendant, I say, a basic foundation of folk is where the lyrics *sincerely* belong,

That place, *where you sir*, put that word in your song.

That time, *when you sir*, wrote "deepest"; a strange, bewildering time.

When, *I put it to you sir* … YOU! … committed a lyrical, comparative, definitional crime.

So we who are *all cuts*, say we wish you'd been less careless, within your writing space,

And on those solid foundations, Milord … we do … rest our case."

O CAT, IT'S JUST so superficial, to think the (comparative) worst,

of what some call initial, but you called … the first.

Maybe you should've thought, and looked, before you did leap.

(But with *caritas*, I will meet you halfway, I concede, a first cut *can* sometimes be deep.)

Although …

        never, ever, ever

                … *comparatively* so.

AND ...

CAT WHAT IS THIS thing you have with Tuesdays?

We know Friday and Saturday are traditionally booze-days.

(Ah Saturday night, another one)

But what has Tuesday ever done?

Monday is the end of the weekend run.

Wednesday is the hump,

Tuesday and Thursday deserve a good pump.

And you declare Tuesday dead!

O Cat, what thin ice, on which, you *heavily* tread.

CAT, IF THE WORLD is so wild,

Surely the child,

has lots of places to play.

Cat, if skyscrapers filled the air today,

it's not so wild, it's ... urban.

So Cat really, what fills out your *metaphorical* turban?

And I'm wondering about making love to that dead lady.

Dead.

Cat, *are you okay?* Has morning broken for you, up there in your head?

IN GENERAL, IT SEEMS wildly inconsistent,

so I am quite persistent …

And genuine, not 'taking the piss',

Because I do … love you … *and* your music, through all of this.

But, you can sit on your own not by yourself, (I can't *even begin* to make sense of that …

are the moon shadows after you, once again, Cat?)

Look after yourself. Love your dog again. Live in a wig-wam,

Or on your own not by yourself with a … tillerman?

What better place than a teepee,

to be right there with him, sharing your tea?

CAT, JUST TAKE this advice in a small rant from me:

I know, you think you see the light, so if you want to sing out, that could be alright.

And, we all know you can see the change a-coming,

But Cat, you *can* keep it in, if you're that itchy to sing, maybe start humming.

Cat, stay, don't change, I mean stay where you are! Don't change from touching Katmandu,

That mystical place, it's just like you,

it's bewildering … strange.

CAT, it's not time, to make a change.

www.ingramcontent.com/pod-product-compliance
Lightning Source LLC
Chambersburg PA
CBHW041414010726
47507CB00005B/269